[SURVIVING
THE IMPOSSIBLE]

SURVIVING
A KILLER
VIRUS

CHARLIE OGDEN

Gareth Stevens
PUBLISHING

Please visit our website, **www.garethstevens.com**.
For a free color catalog of all our high-quality books,
call toll free 1-800-542-2595 or fax 1-877-542-2596.

Cataloging-in-Publication Data
Names: Ogden, Charlie.
Title: Surviving a killer virus / Charlie Ogden.
Description: New York : Gareth Stevens Publishing, 2018. | Series: Surviving the impossible | Includes index.
Identifiers: ISBN 9781538214633 (pbk.) | ISBN 9781538214169 (library bound) | ISBN 9781538214640 (6 pack)
Subjects: LCSH: Virus diseases--Juvenile literature. | Epidemics--Juvenile literature. |
    Communicable diseases -- Juvenile literature. | Disasters--Juvenile literature. | Survival--Juvenile literature.
Classification: LCC RA644.V55 O43 2018 | DDC 614.5'8--dc2

Published in 2018 by
Gareth Stevens Publishing
111 East 14th Street, Suite 349
New York, NY 10003

Copyright © 2018 BookLife

Written by: Charlie Ogden
Edited by: Kirsty Holmes
Designed by: Drue Rintoul

Photo credits: Abbreviations: l–left, r–right, b–bottom, t–top, c–centre, m–middle. Images are courtesy of
Shutterstock.com. With thanks to Getty Images, Thinkstock Photo and iStockphoto.Cover: bg – Adisa, gloves –
Tonhom1009, book – Krechowicz. 2 – Pixus. 3 – Kwanbenz. 4t – Antlio. 5 – Oleg Golovnev. 6b – gmstockstudio.
7 – Evgeny Karandaev. 8 – Vadim Sadovski. 9 – Stokkete. 10t – Pakhnyushchy. 10b – Naeblys. 11r – By Pikawil
from Laval, Canada (Otakuthon 2014: Plague doctor) [CC BY–SA 2.0 (http://creativecommons.org/licenses/
by–sa/2.0)], via Wikimedia Commons. 11bl – Cosmin Manci. 12l – JPC–PROD. 12br – Thanapun. 13t – Alberto
Zornetta. 13b – tommaso79. 14t – Taigi. 15t – Valentina Razumova. 15b – Dudarev Mikhail. 16l – Inked Pixels.
16r – AlenKadr. 17t – 7th Son Studio. 18l – Michel Cecconi. 18r – sittipong. 19t – Aaron Amat, Tim UR, Sergiy
Kuzmin, jules2000, Arunas Gabalis. 19b – My Life Graphic, Kamenetskiy Konstantin, design56. 20t – Andrei
Orlov. 20b – Fotokostic. 21 – Alexander Smulskiy. 22t – grop. 22b – Valentyn Volkov. 23 – Stenko Vlad. 23bl
– Fotofermer. 24t – sirtravelalot. 24b – michaelheim. 25r – file404. 25l – nevodka. 26b – WAYHOME studio.
27 – Mary Rice. 28t – Tarasenko Andrey. 28b – littleny. 29 – Brian Kinney. 30t – Guy J. Sagi. 30b – 9nong.

Printed in China

CPSIA compliance information: Batch CW18GS: For further information contact
Gareth Stevens, New York, New York at 1-800-542-2595.

CONTENTS

Page 4   **Killer Viruses**

Page 6   **The Outbreak**

Page 8   **Know Your Pandemic**

Page 14   **Avoiding Contamination**

Page 18   **Choosing a Hideout**

Page 22   **Gathering Supplies**

Page 26   **Finding the Cure**

Page 30   **Surviving the Killer Virus**

Page 31   **Glossary**

Page 32   **Index**

Words that look like THIS can be found in the glossary on page 31.

KILLER VIRUSES

We're all scared of murderers, assassins, and killers. And we're right to be scared. These AGENTS of evil would take your life in a heartbeat and not give it a second thought.

However, some killers are scarier than others – and the most frightening killer of all is the one that no one can see and that no one seems able to stop. Unlike murderers and assassins, a killer virus can sneak up on you and get inside you without you knowing. And once that has happened, you're as good as dead.

BIOLOGICAL EVIL

A killer virus is a **BIOLOGICAL** agent of evil. It's just as brutal as Jack the Ripper or any other murderer, and it is able to kill thousands more people. It can't be seen or heard and, until a **CURE** is found, it can't be stopped – you can't lock a killer virus up in prison. Once a killer virus gets inside a body, or a "host," it can make copies of itself over and over again. Within only a few hours, a virus can copy itself a million times and **INFECT** every last inch of your body.

THE OUTBREAK

When a killer virus starts to take over the world, you can bet that people will notice. A killer virus can spread fast – sweeping across an entire country at amazing speeds. This means surviving a killer virus really is a race against time.

If you're one of the lucky ones, you'll hear about the PANDEMIC before it gets to your country, town, or city. You might hear about the virus on the news – if the news reporter doesn't drop down dead in the middle of the announcement, that is.

TECHNICAL DIFFICULTIES PLEASE STAND BY

Your best chance at finding out about the killer virus pandemic is through the internet. On the internet, anyone can write a blog or post a video explaining what's going on in their town. More importantly, it only takes a few minutes to do. So even if a person only has a few minutes to live, they can still share their news with the world using the internet.

Top Tip: Television stations and newspapers might not report on the virus in an attempt to stop people from panicking. However, it's very hard to hide the truth from the internet.

KNOW YOUR PANDEMIC

Facing a killer virus pandemic is one of the scariest things that the world can come up against. However; some killer viruses are easier to face than others. If you're lucky, the killer virus will be one that spreads slowly, but kills its victims quickly. This way the victims will be dead before they can pass it on, and HUMANITY has a chance to survive.

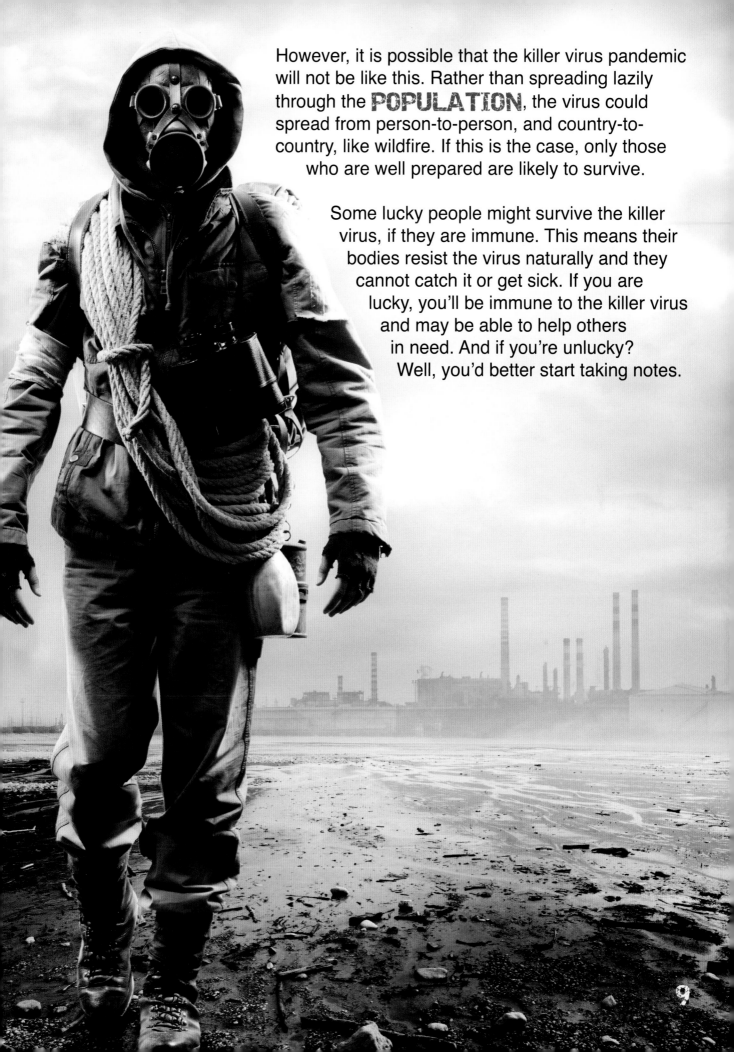

However, it is possible that the killer virus pandemic will not be like this. Rather than spreading lazily through the **POPULATION**, the virus could spread from person-to-person, and country-to-country, like wildfire. If this is the case, only those who are well prepared are likely to survive.

Some lucky people might survive the killer virus, if they are immune. This means their bodies resist the virus naturally and they cannot catch it or get sick. If you are lucky, you'll be immune to the killer virus and may be able to help others in need. And if you're unlucky? Well, you'd better start taking notes.

9

The bubonic plague is one of history's most famous killers. This is not only because it killed a lot of people, but also because it kept coming back again and again, killing more people every few hundred years.

This **MICROSCOPIC** killer first attacked humanity back in the Middle Ages. It started in Egypt, then it was spread by rats and fleas through Europe. It killed almost a quarter of the population: 25 million people!

Egypt

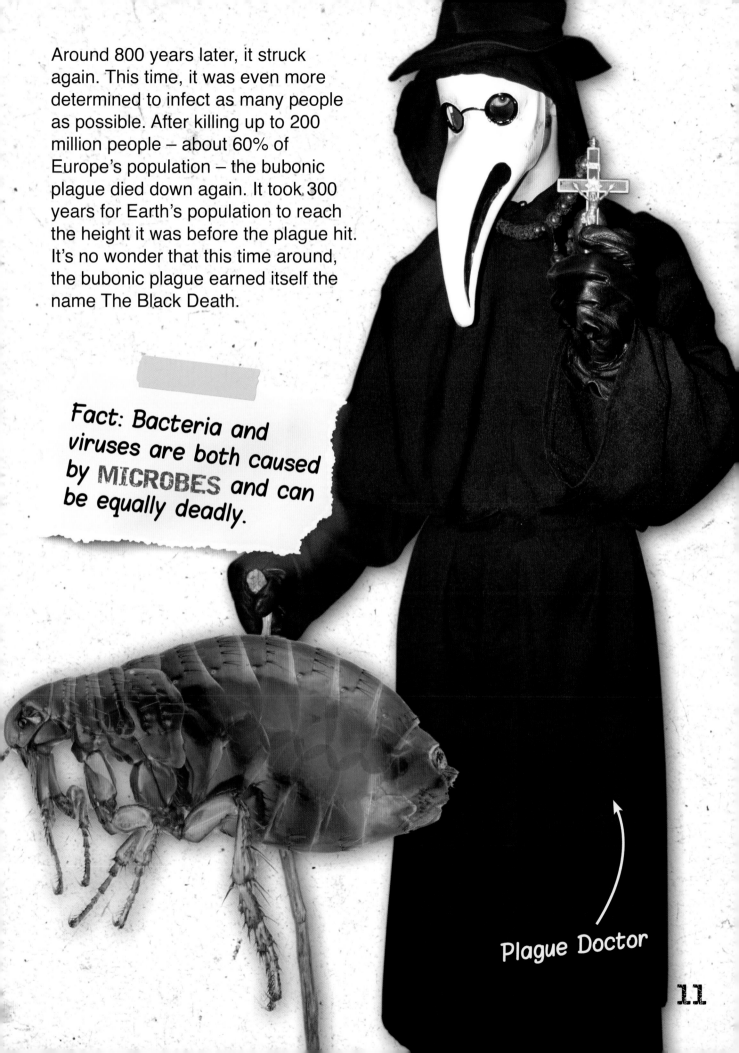

Around 800 years later, it struck again. This time, it was even more determined to infect as many people as possible. After killing up to 200 million people – about 60% of Europe's population – the bubonic plague died down again. It took 300 years for Earth's population to reach the height it was before the plague hit. It's no wonder that this time around, the bubonic plague earned itself the name The Black Death.

Fact: Bacteria and viruses are both caused by MICROBES and can be equally deadly.

Plague Doctor

SYMPTOMS

A virus can kill in a lot of different ways. The ways that a virus affects the body and the mind are known as symptoms – and with killer viruses, each symptom is more gruesome than the last. Here is a short list of symptoms that could be caused by the world's next killer virus.

COUGHING BLOOD

If you start coughing blood, you'll know that something isn't right. This symptom alone probably won't kill you, but it's a sign that your body is fighting against a terrible illness – and losing.

EXPLODING BOILS

This was one the main symptoms of the bubonic plague which, as we know, really knew how to destroy the human body. If pus–filled, swollen boils start bursting from your skin, you could be in big trouble.

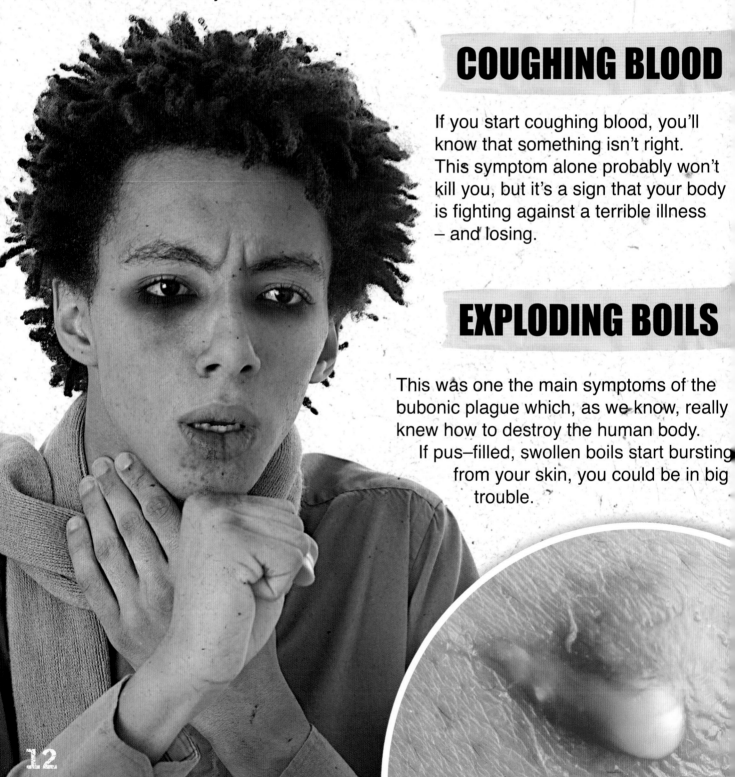

INSANITY

Any virus that makes its way into the brain is bad. Very bad. A killer virus could do all sorts of damage up there. It could twist your thoughts, bend your mind, and leave you in serious trouble. If you're lucky, you might go so mad that you don't even realize that a killer virus is infecting all your friends and family.

PARALYSIS

Paralysis is almost like the opposite of insanity – your mind stays active, but your body becomes completely unable to move. However, being locked inside your own head, incapable of lifting a finger or twitching your lips, can make almost anyone go insane.

AVOIDING CONTAMINATION

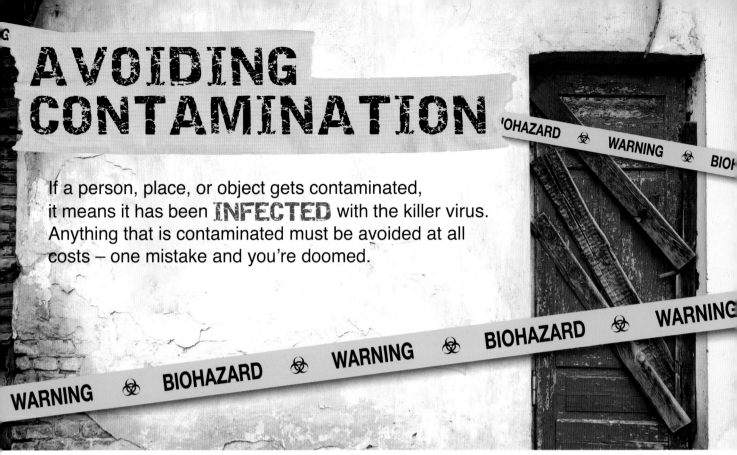

If a person, place, or object gets contaminated, it means it has been **INFECTED** with the killer virus. Anything that is contaminated must be avoided at all costs – one mistake and you're doomed.

WHAT TO AVOID

Two of the most common things to get contaminated are food and water. Once a virus gets into a **WATER SUPPLY**, it can spread quickly from place to place. Most of the water on Earth is connected and because of this, there are very few places on Earth that a virus couldn't contaminate if it spread through water.

Let's say that the water supply in a small area is contaminated. Will you be okay if you just avoid drinking the water? No – you won't. If the water supply in an area is contaminated, it may well be that all the food in that area is contaminated too. All food that comes from plants – vegetables, fruits, nuts, beans, you name it – needs water to grow. If this water is contaminated, then you can bet the food will be too.

Top Tip: Don't think that meat is any safer than fruit and vegetables. Some killer viruses affect humans but not animals. Because of this, animals may be contaminated with the killer virus and not look the slightest bit sick.

HOW IT SPREADS

So, you want to avoid contamination. An important thing to figure out, then, is how the killer virus is spreading. Viruses can move between different people and places in a variety of ways. If you're lucky, the killer virus will only be able to spread in one way. If you're unlucky, it might be able to spread in all of the following ways.

WATER

We know viruses can get in the water. So to avoid the killer virus sneaking into you this way, think before drinking, washing, brushing your teeth or washing your food. There could be a killer virus in every deadly drop. Try to find bottled water from before the outbreak, or you're not going to make it.

Contaminated insects are harder to avoid. If the killer virus is carried by insects, a single bite could be enough to infect you. If you've ever tried to swat a fly or squash a mosquito, you know just how hard those buzzing bugs are to control. Your best bet in this situation is to go somewhere cold – very cold. Most insects can only survive in   , so pack a couple of extra sweaters and start making your way to the North Pole.

AIR

Viruses can also spread through the air. If this happens – well, you'll be very lucky to avoid contamination. You suck air into your body all day, every day. So if even just one breath of air is contaminated with the killer virus, you're a goner. If someone who is infected coughs or sneezes near you, that could be the end of everything. Because of this, the best way to avoid contamination is by avoiding everyone and everything that could be pumping out virus–filled air. However, this is easier said than done.

CHOOSING A HIDEOUT

Making sure that you find yourself a good HIDEOUT is of utmost importance during a virus pandemic. Knowing how the virus spreads will help you determine what kind of hideout is best. For example, if the virus spreads through insect bites, any hideout in the TROPICS is a no–go. What you really want in that situation is a cozy little igloo somewhere in Alaska.

CONTAMINATIO
FREE
ZONE

BUNKER LIFE

However, there are some hideouts that will help you avoid contamination no matter what. One such hideout is a completely sealed **BUNKER** – a place where no water, insects, or air can get in from the outside. This can help you avoid the virus but you won't be able to survive without fresh air and water for very long. Luckily, bunkers like this are full of gadgets and gizmos, including machines that can clean the air and devices that can turn your pee back into drinking water – if you're brave enough to drink it, that is.

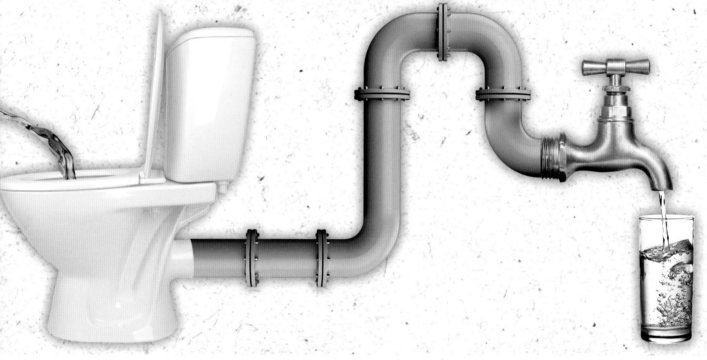

However, even the most high–tech bunkers won't have the technology to make food out of nothing. Because of this, your bunker is going to need to be stocked with enough food to last you the entire pandemic – which could last decades. You need to go on a pretty big shopping trip! Secondly, there are only a handful of these bunkers scattered across the world. Odds are, you have no idea where any of them are.

GET AWAY FROM IT ALL

As bunkers are few and far between, you might have to start thinking about hideouts that are within your reach. The most important thing you need to think about here is location – you need to be far, far away from everything that might lead to you getting infected.

The best hideout for surviving a killer virus pandemic is one that is many miles from the nearest town, person or animal. Without any people or animals around, your chances of getting infected are much lower.

Once you've found your desert island hideout – or somewhere that is equally remote – you can start living your new life! To begin with, it will mostly involve gathering supplies, farming, and collecting water. After that, it will probably involve more gathering supplies, more farming, and more water collecting. No one said that surviving a killer virus pandemic would be fun or easy, but at least you're surviving.

Top Tip: While you are looking for your hideout, be sure to keep the seeds from any fruits or vegetables that you eat. You can use these later to grow your own food.

GATHERING SUPPLIES

In order to make it through the killer virus pandemic, you're going to need to collect enough food, water and supplies to last at least a few months. While gathering your supplies, you need to do everything you can to avoid being contaminated by the virus. The best way to do this is to avoid towns and cities and look for supplies in the **WILDERNESS**.

When looking for food in the wilderness, there's one thing you need to remember – don't eat anything you don't recognize. Eating the wrong piece of fruit could make you just as sick as if you caught the virus! So, no matter how hungry you get, stay away from mysterious-looking berries – or they might end up being your last meal.

Finding clean water can be just as hard as finding food – if not harder. If you stumble across a stream or river with clear water, the best thing to do is to collect some and boil it, as this will kill any bacteria. Make a small fire, fill a metal container with water – an old can of beans works just as well as a saucepan – and heat the water until bubbles rise from the bottom and it begins to boil. The heat from the fire should kill any traces of the killer virus that might have contaminated the water, as well as any other nasty things that might be in there.

Top Tip: After you've boiled the water, it may still taste bad even if it's clean. An easy way to fix this is by adding a tea bag and making a cup of tea.

supplies – and lots of them. Getting your hands on medical supplies will help you avoid contamination. If you are feeling like a hero, you can even treat those around you who have been infected and keep them from passing the killer disease on to you!

Nearly all medical supplies will be useful to you, so leave nothing behind when you're rummaging through medicine cupboards and first aid kits. However, some medical supplies are more important than others.

Surgical masks will help you to avoid breathing in any air that has been contaminated with the killer virus. They will also stop those with the virus from contaminating others with their coughing, spluttering and sneezing.

Top Tip: Don't forget to pick up some bug spray! Covering yourself in the stuff should help to ward off any insects that are carrying the killer virus.

FINDING THE CURE

After a few months, years, or decades, the killer virus will eventually begin to die down and fade away. If you're still alive at this point – congratulations! However, the killer virus isn't gone just yet and the battle is far from over.

At this point, there will be small pockets of survivors all over the world. These people will mostly either have managed to avoid contamination or will have been one of the lucky few to be naturally immune to the virus. However, don't let your guard down just yet. Even people who are immune could still be carriers of the virus.

CARRIERS

If someone gets infected with the killer virus and survives – either by some miracle or because they are immune – then they might end up as carriers. Carriers are not sick themselves, but the virus is still inside them, meaning that they can still infect others. As there will still be traces of the virus in some parts of the world and a number of carriers walking around, it will still be unsafe for survivors to meet up. First, you need to find the cure.

SAFETY

MONK

DO NOT ENTER
NO OUTSIDERS
ALLOWED

FINDING SCIENTISTS

Now that the virus has died down and there are only a few people left who can infect you with the virus, it should be safe enough to start exploring the world and looking for the cure. Sure, it will be risky, but someone has to do it! Once the cure has been found, survivors from around the world can come together and humanity can start to REBUILD the post-viral world.

Your best chance at finding the cure is to go to important science LABORATORIES and hospitals. Many of these buildings will be empty and abandoned, but a few will hopefully be home to some scientists who have survived the pandemic and are working on a cure. These places might take a while to find, but the human race is counting on you – so don't give up!

You will have learned a lot about the virus by now. Help the scientists to figure out how it works. This will help them cure it. This could also take a long time, but it's important work, so keep at it! It will only be a matter of time before you make a breakthrough and the killer virus will be defeated once and for all.

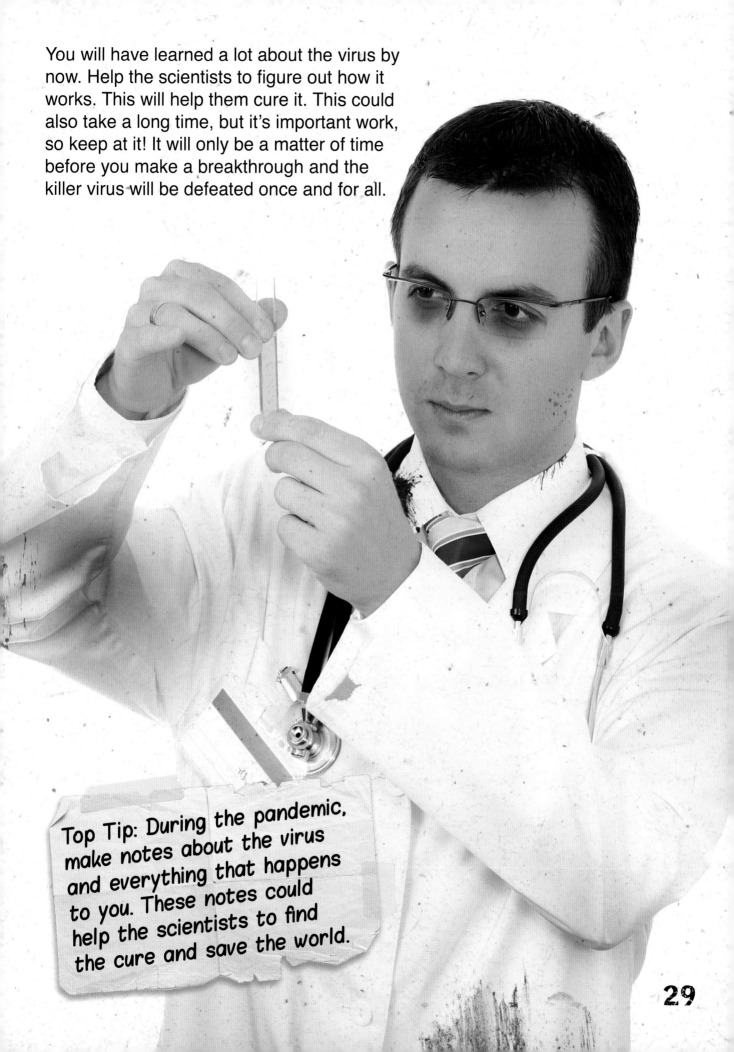

Top Tip: During the pandemic, make notes about the virus and everything that happens to you. These notes could help the scientists to find the cure and save the world.

SURVIVING THE KILLER VIRUS

Once the cure has been found, you can start to bring survivors together and rebuild the world.
Use a radio signal or the internet to send a message to the world.
Tell everyone that the killer virus cure has been found!
Let the world know where you are, and soon all those who survived the pandemic will arrive.

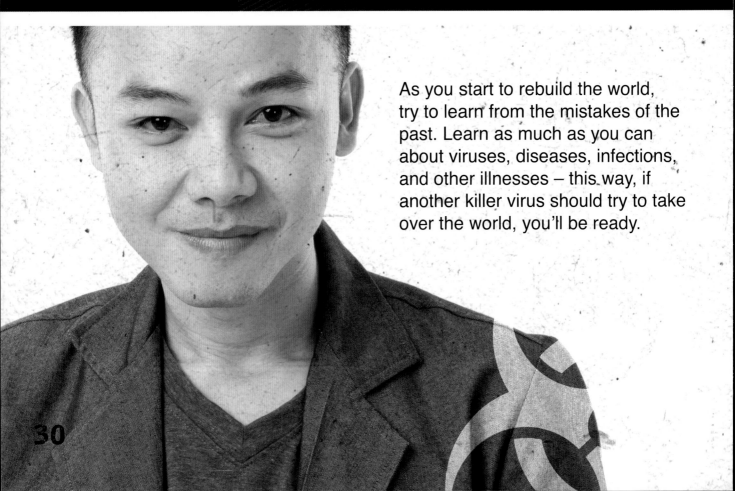

As you start to rebuild the world, try to learn from the mistakes of the past. Learn as much as you can about viruses, diseases, infections, and other illnesses – this way, if another killer virus should try to take over the world, you'll be ready.

GLOSSARY

AGENTS — people or things that produce specific effects

BIOLOGICAL — relating to living things

BUNKER — an underground shelter that contains everything needed for a few people to survive for a few years

CURE — a substance or treatment that takes away the symptoms of a virus and makes a person healthy again

HIDEOUT — a safe building that can be used as a base during an emergency

HUMANITY — all human beings, as a group

INFECT — contaminate or affect a person with a disease or virus

INFECTED — a person who has been contaminated with a virus and is showing symptoms

LABORATORIES — a room or building that has the technology needed to perform scientific experiments

MICROBES — tiny living things made from a single cell, including bacteria, viruses and fungi

MICROSCOPIC — so small that it cannot be seen with the naked eye

PANDEMIC — an outbreak of a disease or virus that has spread across most of the world

POPULATION — the amount of people living in a certain area

REBUILD — to restore something that has been damaged or destroyed

TROPICS — the warm and wet part of the world around the Equator

WARM CLIMATES — places that are moderately hot and are usually home to insects

WATER SUPPLY — a source of water for a building or town, such as a well

WILDERNESS — a region where no people live and that is often covered in plant life

INDEX

agents of evil 4

air 17, 19, 25

Black Death 11

blood 12

bodies 5, 12-13, 17

bubonic plague 10-12

bunkers 19, 20

carriers 26-27

contamination 14-17, 19, 22-26

coughing 6, 10

countries 12, 17, 25

cure 5, 26-30

doctors 11

Europe 10-11

fleas 10

food 14-16, 19, 21-24

hideouts 18-21

immunity 5, 11, 13-14, 17, 20, 24, 27-28, 30

infection 9, 26, 27

insanity 13

insects 17-19, 25

internet 7, 30

laboratories 6, 8-9, 13, 16-17, 19, 26

luck 28

medicine 24

microscopic 10

mosquitoes 17

news 6-7

notes 9, 29

outbreak 6, 16

pandemic 6-10, 18-22, 28-29

paralysis 13

plague 10-12

population 9-11

rats 11

scientists 5, 28-29

spread 6-10, 14, 16-18

supplies 21-22, 24

survivors 26-28, 30

symptoms 12

washing 16

water 14-16, 19, 21-24

wilderness 22